The Night Before Christmas

Written by Clement C. Moore
Illustrated by Bernadine Stetzel

PRGOTT BOOKS Publishing

Norway, Maine

www.prgottbooks.net

The Night Before Christmas

Written by Clement C. Moore (1779-1863)
Illustrated by Bernadine Stetzel

Layout by Laura Ashton *laura.ashton@gitflorida.com*

ISBN 978-1491252147

Printed in the United States of America

PRGott Books Publishing

Dedicated to
my loving and
beautiful Grandchildren

and to all
children everywhere.

I have not illustrated the "Night before Christmas" in the usual Victorian style. Instead I have illustrated it in my father's birthplace and surrounding area.

The Puffenbergers were the first settlers in Liberty township in Seneca County, Ohio.

The house and the furnishings were described to me by my father in his 84th year, 3 months befor his death.

THe Night Before Christmas

by Clement C. Moore

illustrated by
B.P. Stetzel

'Twas the night
before Christmas
when all through
the house
Not a creature was
stirring,
not even a mouse.

The stockings were
hung by the chimney
with care

In hopes that **Saint Nicholas**

soon would be there.

The children were
nestled all snug in their beds,

while visions
of sugarplums
danced in their heads.

And Mamma in her
kerchief and I in my
cap
Had just settled down
for a long winter's nap,

When out on the lawn there
arose such a clatter,
I sprang from my bed to see
what was the matter.
Away to the window I flew
like a flash,
Tore open the shutters and
Threw up the sash.

B.P.S.

The moon on the breast of the
new- fallen snow
Gave a luster of midday to
objects below,
When what to my wondering eyes
should appear,
But a miniature sleigh and eight
tiny reindeer,

with a little old driver
so lively and quick,
I Knew in a
moment it
must be
Saint Nick.

More rapid than eagles
his coursers they came,
and he whistled, and shouted
and called them by name:

To the top of the porch,
to the top of the wall!
Now, dash away!
Dash away!
Dash away, all!"

As dry leaves that before
the wild hurricane fly,
When they meet with an
obstacle, mount to the sky,
So up to the housetop the
coursers they flew
With a sleigh full of toys
and saint Nicholas too.

B.P.S

And then in a twinkling
I heard on the roof

The prancing and
pawing
of each little hoof.

As I drew in my head and was
turning around,
Down the chimney **Saint**

Nicholas came with a bound.
He was dressed all in fur
from his head to his foot,
And his clothes were all
tarnished with ashes and soot.

B.P.S.

A bundle of toys
he had flung
    on his back,
And he looked like
a peddler just
opening his pack.

B.P.S.

His eyes– how they twinkled!
His dimples– how merry!

His cheeks were like
roses,
his nose like a
cherry!

B.P.S.

His dress little mouth
was drawn up like a bow,
And the beard on his chin
was as white as the snow.

The stump of a pipe he held
tight in his teeth,
And the smoke it encircled
his head like a
wreath.

B.P.S

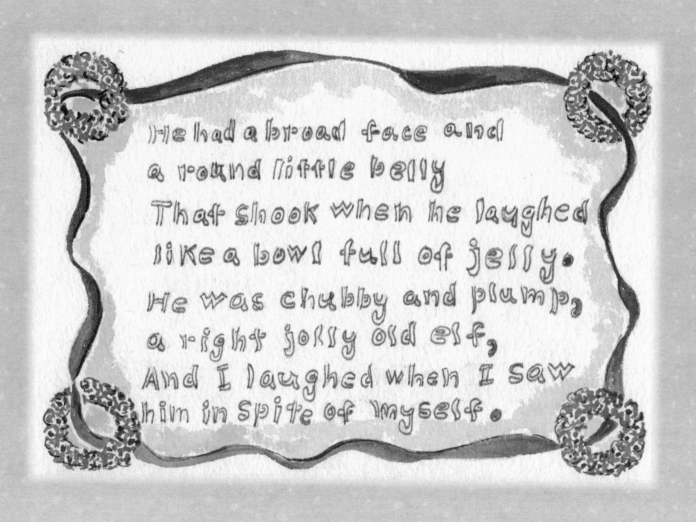

He had a broad face and
a round little belly
That shook when he laughed
like a bowl full of jelly.
He was chubby and plump,
a right jolly old elf,
And I laughed when I saw
him in spite of myself.

With a wink of his eye
and a twist of his head
soon gave me to know
I had nothing to dread.

He spoke not a word
but went straight
to his work

And filled all the stockings;
then turned with a jerk,

And laying his finger
aside of his nose,
And giving a nod,
up the chimney he rose.

He sprang to his sleigh,
And away they all flew
But I heard him exclaim

"HAPPY

to all and to

to his team gave a whistle,
like the down of a thistle.
ere he drove out of sight,

CHRISTMAS

all a good night!"

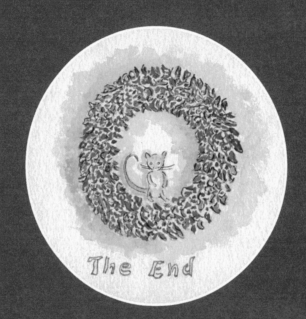

The End

Author's Comments

In most versions of **The Night Before Christmas** that I have seen, the home that St. Nicholas visits is always a big Victorian house. I decided that if Saint Nicholas could visit a fancy Victorian home than why he couldn't visit a little log house in the country as well. Thus the reason I created a log house for my setting of **The Night Before Christmas**.

My father was born in a log house in 1895. In 1980 I sat down with him and asked him to describe the house and what went on inside. His description of the log house is what I based my illustrations on.

My fifth great-grandfather built the log house in 1840. There were four generations born there, including my grandfather from whom I inherited my artistic and creative ability. My grandfather was not only an artist but he built furniture, repaired watches, and farmed. He designed and built all the furniture inside the log house at the time he and my grandmother occupied it. My illustrations depict the exterior and interior of the house at the time my grandparents and their children lived there.

Bernadine Stetzel